RACING AGAINST TIME

Writer and teacher Chris Cooper
lives in Wisconsin, in the United
States, with a big family and
lots of animals.

TRAMP

RACING AGAINST TIME

Chris Cooper

Illustrated by Stephen Player

PUFFIN

PUFFIN BOOKS

Published by the Penguin Group
Penguin Books Ltd, 80 Strand, London WC2R 0RL, England
Penguin Group (USA) Inc., 375 Hudson Street, New York, New York 10014, USA
Penguin Books Australia Ltd, 250 Camberwell Road, Camberwell, Victoria 3124, Australia
Penguin Books Canada Ltd, 10 Alcorn Avenue, Toronto, Ontario, Canada M4V 3B2
Penguin Books India (P) Ltd, 11 Community Centre, Panchsheel Park, New Delhi – 110 017, India
Penguin Group (NZ), cnr Airborne and Rosedale Roads, Albany, Auckland 1310, New Zealand
Penguin Books (South Africa) (Pty) Ltd, 24 Sturdee Avenue, Rosebank 2196, South Africa

Penguin Books Ltd, Registered Offices: 80 Strand, London WC2R 0RL, England

www.penguin.com

First published 2004
1

Text copyright © Chris Cooper, 2004
Illustrations copyright © Stephen Player, 2004
All rights reserved

The moral right of the author and illustrator has been asserted

Set in 14/19 pt Bembo

Made and printed in England by Clays Ltd, St Ives plc

British Library Cataloguing in Publication Data
A CIP catalogue record for this book is available from the British Library

ISBN 0-141-30965-2

For my mum

Tramp's old life seems like a dream – playing in the garden, running in the park, sleeping in front of the fire and, most of all, being with his beloved master, Joe. But when Joe saw Tramp being swept away by the black waters of an underground river, he thought that his best friend had gone forever. Now Tramp must make the long journey home. The road ahead of him seems endless, but he knows that every weary step brings him closer to Joe, closer to home …

Chapter 1

Winter had arrived and the days were at their shortest. By the time Tramp saw lights up ahead, it had been dark for a few hours. A small flame of hope sparked inside the dog at the sight of those lights – perhaps he'd find a place to rest and shelter from the cold there? – but it was hard to keep that hope alive. As night had fallen, so had the temperature. The chill wind buffeted him, and the dog's back leg ached more than ever. The occasional flake of snow in the air hinted at even worse weather on the way.

Pushing through the pain and the tiredness, Tramp continued towards the glow of the electric lights.

It wasn't easy to be cold and alone like this again. The dog had been forced to delay his long journey several weeks earlier, when his back leg had been fractured. Luckily for Tramp, Judy, a volunteer for the local animal shelter and a true dog lover, had taken him in. He had grown accustomed to being well fed and warm at her house while his leg mended.

And yet, Tramp couldn't shake the restless feeling at the back of his mind. Judy was a great owner, but she wasn't *his* owner. She was kind and loving to him, but she was that way to all dogs. That's why Judy volunteered to act as a 'foster owner' for any dogs at the shelter that needed special attention. Every time Tramp found himself relaxing and starting to enjoy life here, an image of his old master, Joe – his true master – would pop into his mind. No, he knew he had to continue on his journey home, just as soon as he could.

At last, the day came when Tramp was taken to the vet's and the splint on his leg removed. He touched the floor gingerly with his back paw. It felt good to walk on all fours once again, even if the muscles of the injured leg felt weak through lack of use.

It was time to move on.

Judy had been sitting in her favourite chair with the newspaper, when Tramp came up to her and pawed her knee.

'You're not looking for more food, are you?' she asked. 'I've never seen a dog eat as much as you did this morning!'

Tramp just looked at this woman who had shown him such kindness. In a rush he leaned forwards and gave her face a lick.

'Get off, you great soppy thing!' laughed Judy.

Tramp wandered out to the garden and out of Judy's line of vision. He looked at the fence ahead of him. He had jumped over this fence once before, but that had been before his back leg had been injured. It might not be so easy now.

Tramp took a breath and charged towards the fence. As before, he sailed over. The instant he landed on the pavement on the other side, he knew that his status had changed. Once more, he was not a pet. He was a stray dog again, trying to find his way home across the miles.

The rest of the day was a blur of sore feet and aching bones and a growing emptiness in his stomach, as Tramp headed west. It didn't take long to leave the town behind him, and then he was crossing open land. A large highway ran straight west, and he kept it in sight as if navigating along the banks of a mighty river.

Knowing that he must find shelter before he could give in to sleep, Tramp carried on long after the sky had darkened. And that's when he saw the lights up ahead . . .

Chapter 2

They belonged to a small café, set back from the highway, and just beyond that a small motel.

Tramp could smell the food from a long way away. Although he had eaten as much as he possibly could at Judy's house that morning, he was back to his usual condition – starving. Perhaps he could find something to eat in the rubbish bins round the back of the café?

But, as he neared the building, the front door opened and someone stepped out. He was young and his long hair was pulled back in a loose ponytail. The light jacket he wore wasn't enough to keep out the cold evening air.

The man had a kind, open face and Tramp thought that it was worth a try to see if he had any food. The dog gave a friendly bark.

'Hey, boy,' said the man, rubbing his hands together to warm them.

Tramp barked again, wagging his tail. Then he sat down expectantly.

The man hesitated, then grinned. 'I get it,' he said. 'It's food you're after, right?'

He opened the plastic container he had been carrying under one arm, and smiled.

'You do realize these leftovers were going to be my lunch for tomorrow?'

He pulled a few strips of bacon out and tossed them to Tramp, who scoffed them down in an instant. They were cold, over

done almost to a crisp, and completely and utterly delicious.

'I guess that's why they call them doggy bags,' laughed the man. He began to walk across the parking lot to the motel that adjoined the café. 'You'd better go home now, doggy,' he said over his shoulder. 'Radio said worse weather's on the way . . .'

Tramp watched as the man entered one of the rooms on the ground level of the motel. Then the dog took up position outside the café entrance. Maybe he would be just as lucky with the next person who came out? He waited and waited, but no one came.

At last, a face did appear at the door. It was a woman, but she didn't come out; she just locked the door from the inside, gave Tramp a suspicious look, and then turned round, clicking off the light at the front of the café. There would be no more food tonight.

Tramp turned his attention to finding a place to sleep. The doorway of the café offered little protection against the wind. Tramp padded round to the side of the building. There was a large rubbish skip here. It wasn't much, but the narrow gap between this and the wall offered a little shelter. Wearily, Tramp crawled in.

It was so cold now that Tramp could hardly get off to sleep. When he finally did drop off, his dreams were shot through with frost and snow.

It wasn't hard for the sound of a door slamming to pull Tramp from this fitful sleep. He opened his eyes. In the distance, the man from the café, the one who had given him some food, was leaving his room. He went along the walkway, pulling change from his pocket, until he reached the vending machine.

Tramp hauled himself out and made his way across the parking lot. The man was heading back to his motel room when he saw the dog.

'What are you doing still out?' the man asked.

Tramp wagged his tail, but he was too cold and tired to muster much of a bark.

A frown clouded the man's face. 'Haven't

you got a home to go to?' he asked.

Tramp took a step closer. The man had a better look at the dog now that he was in the light.

'I don't think you do,' he murmured thoughtfully. He glanced in the direction of the motel lobby. 'What they don't know won't hurt them,' he said at last. 'Come on.'

Tramp followed him along the walkway. The man unlocked the door to his room and held it open for Tramp. The dog padded into the warmth of the small room. He instantly settled into a corner.

'Just don't bark,' said the man, making sure the curtains were completely drawn so that no one might spot the extra guest in the room.

Tramp was half asleep when the light was clicked off. Seconds later he heard the sound of bed springs as the man sat up.

'Hey!' hissed a voice from across the room, and Tramp could almost feel its grin in the dark. 'You don't snore, do you?'

Chapter 3

Tramp's journey had been a long, hard trek. Apart from stops to rest or eat, his entire existence consisted of the exhausting task of just keeping going, of putting one paw in front of the other, hour after hour.

But the next day was different. Tramp travelled in style! After an early (and hasty) breakfast, the man, who said that his name was Jimmy, loaded his one bag into the boot of the little car parked outside. The car had seen better days – its body was mottled with dents and patches of rust. There were stickers across the rear bumper and the bottom of the back window.

Tramp waited patiently and watched the man.

'You sure you haven't got an owner?' asked Jimmy, at last. Then he shrugged.

'Well, you're not the usual sort of hitch-hiker, but I could use some company for the rest of the trip,' he said. He opened the passenger door. 'You talked me into it!' he said.

Tramp didn't follow much of what the man was saying, but he knew better than to turn down an offer like this. He hopped into the car and settled himself on the front seat. The floor was covered with sweet wrappers and styrofoam cups.

'Excuse the mess,' said Jimmy as he started up the car. And then they were off! Once they had joined the highway, Tramp knew they were going in the right direction because the morning sun lay behind them.

Jimmy kept a woolly hat pulled over his ears as he drove. He didn't have gloves on, but he'd pulled the sleeves of his sweatshirt down to cover his hands.

'Heater doesn't work too well,' he said to his uncomprehending passenger. 'But the radio does!'

Jimmy spent a few minutes searching for a song he liked. When he found one he turned it up good and loud. Tramp just looked out of the side window as mile after mile slipped by, each one a mile closer to home.

'What should we call you, anyway?' shouted Jimmy, looking across at the passenger seat. He noticed that the dog's tail was wagging away. It seemed to be keeping time with the beat of the music from the radio.

'Got it!' exclaimed Jimmy. 'We'll call you "Rocker", yeah?'

They drove on. After a while, they stopped to get petrol and Jimmy bought snacks for them to eat on the way. He added to the mound of empty packets and wrappers that littered the car's interior.

'Gotta keep an eye on how much I spend,' said Jimmy. 'I can't really afford this whole trip, but I just couldn't resist dropping in on my sister and her family for the holidays. It'll freak her out!' He grinned at the thought. 'If we make good time, we should get there later on tonight.'

Tramp was content to let the man chat away to him. Every so often, Jimmy would let out a yell of recognition when they played a favourite of his on the radio.

It was still early when they stopped for dinner, though it was already dark. Jimmy bought a burger, which he shared with Tramp, and a portion of French fries, which he wolfed down himself. There was just time for Jimmy to nip to the fast food restaurant's toilets, and for Tramp to nip to the patch of wasteland behind the building for the same reason, and then they were back on the road.

As the evening wore on, there was less and less traffic on the road. Despite the cold, Jimmy had cracked a side window open to keep the car from fogging up. It began to snow, lightly at first, but then more strongly. The car's windscreen wipers were on, but they only worked on the intermittent setting and it was hard to see very far ahead. The screen filled with flakes between each swish of the wipers.

Jimmy slowed down. 'Hoped we'd beat the snow,' he muttered, leaning forwards against the steering wheel and peering ahead.

But Tramp had other things on his mind. An odd feeling had crept up on him – slowly at first, but as the minutes and miles went by, he became more and more certain of it.

It was this – he was nearing his home!

No human could know how Tramp knew this. It was a unique combination of smells in the air, smells that only a dog could identify. Taken together, they were as recognizable to a dog as a picture might be to you or me . . . With a jolt of excited anticipation, Tramp realized that he must be no more than a day's journey from home – less time than that in a car! He might be reunited with Joe sooner than he'd ever imagined!

Tramp could hardly sit still as the notion gripped him. His long, hard journey across the country might soon be over! He let out a little bark of joy.

'Oh, you like this song, do you?' asked Jimmy, reaching for the volume control on the radio. 'Me too! It's an oldie but goodie.' He turned up the music until they could feel the bass rumbling through their chests, with Jimmy singing along to the chorus – 'Baby, we were born to run!' – and Tramp joining in with a bark every so often.

The music was thumping away as they passed a police car parked in the central reservation between the westbound and eastbound lanes of the highway. The song had finished as they rounded a bend in the road. A DJ on the radio began chattering away. Impatiently, Jimmy bent down to find a different station with less talk.

'Jabber, jabber, jabber . . . I say cut the waffle! We need more music and less talk,' he said. 'Right, Rocker?'

But then everything went very, very wrong.

The car hit a patch of ice on the slick surface. The back wheels swung out wide, as if with a mind of their own. Jimmy jerked upright, pulling both hands on to the steering wheel again, but it was too late. The car was spinning out of control. Tramp was suddenly aware that the constant background noise of the tyres on the road had become a rumble. The car was bouncing up and down as it sped across rougher terrain. It had left the hard shoulder and was barrelling down the ravine that ran alongside this stretch of the highway.

Tramp just had time to see the trees ahead, stern and silent in the snow, and then there was a terrible sound of metal crumpling and glass shattering as the car struck something, a jolt of pain, and Tramp fell into unconsciousness.

Chapter 4

He woke to blackness. The car's engine was silent, but the radio still let out a hiss of static. Urgently, Tramp sniffed at the figure slumped forwards in the driver's seat. Jimmy was not moving and Tramp could smell blood, but he could also hear the low rasp of the man's breath.

The side window next to Tramp had smashed as the front end of the car crumpled in on itself. It was difficult in the cramped space, but Tramp managed to turn himself around and wriggle through the gap.

Chunks of glass dug into the pads of his front paws, but he ignored them.

Snow was still falling, but not much had settled on the ground yet. Tramp ran back up the embankment to the highway. Once he reached the hard shoulder, he looked back. Through the swirl of falling snow and in the darkness of the ravine, it was hard to spot the crashed car.

There were no lights visible anywhere, nothing Tramp could do but wait until another vehicle passed by. But it was late by now and the dog had a long wait. He stood trembling in the cold. Part of him wanted to rush back down to the car and see how the man was, but he forced himself to stay at the road. The falling snow had soon covered the tyre tracks that led off the road.

At last Tramp heard the sound of an approaching car. Moments later headlights appeared.

Tramp went right up to the edge of the hard shoulder and began to bark for all he was worth. The driver just beeped the horn – perhaps to make sure the dog didn't run out into the highway – and moved the car out into the overtaking lane. As it whizzed past, Tramp began to charge in the same direction, still barking. He glimpsed a pale face in the passenger seat looking back at him, and then the car was gone and all he could see was the red glow of its rear lights in the snow.

The road was deserted again. How long before another car went by? And when it did, why wouldn't it too simply speed by? Tramp didn't know what to do, he –

The police car!

The police car hadn't been far back down the road. Just around the bend, in fact.

Tramp began to trot back along the hard shoulder. He hadn't gone far, when he saw a flash of red and blue lights rounding the bend and heading this way. This was even better – the police car was coming to him!

It was going slowly and it stopped altogether when it caught Tramp in the glare of its headlights. A police officer got out on the passenger side.

'There it is, just like the caller said!' he shouted back to the driver, and then to Tramp, 'Come here!'

Tramp knew that he had to lead them to Jimmy's car. He let out a short bark.

'COME HERE!' shouted the officer, more impatient this time. 'You're going to cause an accident!'

He walked towards the dog with a flashlight in his hand, and the car, lights still flashing, crawled along the hard shoulder behind him. Making sure that the man never got close enough to grab him, Tramp trotted ahead.

'Stupid dog,' muttered the police officer irritably.

When he was near the right spot, Tramp veered off the road. The policeman went to follow him, but then a voice called from inside the police car: 'Let it go! It probably lives on a farm near here. We'll never catch it!'

The first police officer turned back. 'You reckon?' He started back to the car.

No! They were going to leave! But they hadn't seen the crashed car! What about Jimmy? Tramp had to do something. Bounding towards the man, he began to bark as loudly and fiercely as he could.

Tramp was not attacking, but in the dark and snow, the policeman didn't know that. He brandished the flashlight like a weapon, while the dog completed a loop around the man, jumping and barking like crazy. Then Tramp headed back off the road.

The other police officer was out of the car now. They realized that this dog wasn't going to just leave. If they didn't do something about it, it would stick around here until it caused an accident on the highway.

Resigned to the task, they tracked Tramp in the beams of the flashlight – 'There it goes! That way!' – until the beam stopped on the crashed car.

'We're too late!' snarled one officer. He turned and ran back to the police car to radio for help, while the other officer went to Jimmy's car.

Tramp stayed back and watched from the first line of trees. The police officer crouched at the side of the car, talking to Jimmy in a low voice. Minutes later, Tramp heard a siren approach and then an ambulance arrived at the side of the road.

The dog looked on with concern as the long-haired man was lifted from the car and put on a stretcher by two paramedics. He

didn't seem to be awake, but his head was rolling from side to side. He was alive!

The dog was so intent on Jimmy's fate that he didn't even notice footsteps behind him. Suddenly a collar of some kind looped around his neck.

'You've caused enough trouble for one night,' said the police officer's gruff voice. And then the dog was being tugged away and there was nothing he could do.

Chapter 5

Like most other children in his school, Joe had found it hard to stop his mind from wandering during the last lesson of the day. For most of the children it was the thought that there were only a few more days before school ended for the winter holidays that made it hard to concentrate. Christmas had always been Joe's favourite time of year, but that wasn't what he was thinking about now.

As he sat alone on the bus home, he leaned his head against the window. A kid in the seat behind him was saying that they'd had snow in the hills not far to the east. The same weather front might be moving their way. That meant they might have a white Christmas this year! The bus was filled with excited talk of sledging and snowball fights.

Joe didn't join in. As usual, he was thinking about Tramp. Before long the New Year would be here. Could he really expect to see the dog again?

A man walking a dog outside caught Joe's eye. He recognized both man and pet immediately. They lived further down Joe's street. He didn't know the man's name, but he was all too familiar with the dog's – Fritz!

The black-and-tan Dobermann had been Tramp's biggest enemy in the neighbourhood. Whenever Joe and Tramp had walked past Fritz's house, the Dobermann would unleash a torrent of savage barks at the smaller dog. Tramp had always responded by pressing himself even closer against Joe's legs. On those unlucky occasions when they had encountered each other in the dog park – the only spot in the area where dogs were allowed to run off their leads - Fritz went out of his way to chase the smaller dog.

Joe watched the big dog now as it tugged its owner towards the dog park. The unfairness of it all struck him again. It had been months since he'd had the chance to take Tramp there.

Mum had already finished work when Joe got home.

'Any emails?' he asked, flinging his school bag aside.

Of course, Mum knew what he was asking about. Ever since they had spotted a dog that looked exactly like Tramp on the television news, they had done as much as they could to track the missing pet down. Joe's mum and dad had called dozens of animal shelters. They had sent emails to several Missing Pets web sites across the country. Mum had even helped Joe to set up a web page so that people could send information about Tramp.

Joe's mum shook her head. There had been no emails, but it was clear that she was excited about something. 'There was a phone call,' she said, 'from the TV station.'

Joe's heart leapt. 'Has someone found Tramp?' he asked anxiously.

'No,' said Mum, 'but there's a news producer at the station who saw the web page. She thinks it's a good story. They want to interview you on the morning news.'

Joe's first reaction was one of nerves – he didn't like talking in front of his class, let alone goodness knows how many TV viewers – but he quickly fought this down. He was willing to do anything that would increase their chances of finding Tramp.

Chapter 6

Joe Robbins would have been astonished to know it, but Tramp was no more than twenty miles away. However, there wasn't much chance that the dog would be getting any closer. He had been brought to an animal shelter and led along a narrow corridor with enclosures on either side.

Tramp was put into one of these. It was quite comfortable in there – there was a bowl of fresh water and a towel on the concrete floor for him to sleep on. He did manage to sleep a little, but his dreams now took him back to his earliest memories of puppyhood. He had been in such an animal shelter when he was very little. He didn't even remember how he had got there. Even though all the shelter workers had been nice, it had been a time of fear and loneliness and confusion for him. That awful mix of feelings had only ended when the Robbins family had come and taken him away from that place. Now he was back in another animal shelter and all those feelings swept back inside him and remained throughout the night.

Daytime came as a relief. As soon as one dog noticed the pale sunlight it let out a bark, and then it seemed as if every other dog in the place joined in. Tramp could hear and smell all the other dogs – there seemed to be at least eight of them – but he was only able to see the one in the enclosure opposite his, a sad-eyed cocker spaniel.

The day passed slowly. Every time a shelter worker brought food or fresh water, they would take the time to chat to each of the dogs, but there were still long stretches in which nothing happened.

Just the sound of the door to this section opening was enough to set off a chorus of barks. This happened in the middle of the morning, and two women walked between the two rows of enclosures.

'And, of course, this is where we keep the dogs, Becca,' the taller woman was saying. 'Don't worry, they won't bark quite so much when they know you,' she added with a laugh. 'Your duties will mostly be in the office, but you might have to help out here sometimes too. It's basically a matter of feeding them, changing the bedding, making sure they've got water. Common sense, really.'

The other woman, Becca, stopped at the enclosure opposite Tramp's and bent down to read the card taped to it.

'Name, Toby, male, six years old,' she read aloud. 'Nice temperament.'

The taller woman, whose name was Lisa, nodded. 'We put that information right there for any family who might want to adopt a pet,' she explained. She reached an arm through the door and stroked the spaniel behind the ear. 'Toby here's a lovely dog – aren't you, Toby? Yes, you are! – but he's quite a bit older than what most families are looking for. You know, people love puppies.' The spaniel had closed his eyes and angled his head so that Lisa's hand was scratching the perfect spot. 'Toby came to us when his owner passed away,' continued Lisa. 'There were no relatives who could take him in, so we've been trying to find a home for him. Haven't we, Toby?'

Becca nodded towards Tramp's enclosure. His card read: Not available for adoption at this time.

'What about this one?' asked Becca.

'Ah well, this is our new arrival,' said Lisa.

'So what happens to him?' asked Becca. 'Well, the county vet will look him over later on today. Once we know he hasn't got rabies or anything nasty like that, we'll be able to clean him up a bit. Then we hold him for five days and hope that someone comes and claims him.' She frowned a little. 'I'd be surprised if anyone *did* come and claim him, to be quite honest. Apparently, he was running loose and caused an accident out on the highway.'

'And what if no one claims him?'

Lisa sighed. 'Well, we do our best to put every unclaimed dog we get in here up for adoption, however long it takes,' she said. 'The only times we can't is if we know a dog's too dangerous to fit into a new home.' She squatted down and gave Tramp an appraising look. 'The report said that this one might be a biter. Of course, it could just be that he was reacting untypically in a stressful situation.

But we'll have to keep an eye on him.'

Lisa got to her feet. 'If a dog doesn't have the right temperament to be placed in a home, we'll still try and keep them here as long as we can. It's only when the place is full up and another dog arrives that we have to face hard decisions about what to do. That's our worst scenario – having to have a dog put down because we're out of space. It doesn't happen often, thank goodness, but that's the absolute worst part of the job. That's why we're going to expand the shelter in the spring – we'll be able to house lots more strays then.'

'But . . . the shelter's full up right now, isn't it?' asked Becca.

'Almost.' A cloud of worry crossed Lisa's face. 'That's why we'll have to keep our fingers crossed that we don't get any new arrivals for a while.'

Chapter 7

Tramp was well fed and comfortable enough at the shelter. The workers there were kind – it was clear that they loved animals – but they were too busy to devote a lot of time to any one dog. The days crept by slowly.

The best part of the day was when he was let out into the dog run outside. Lisa or one of the other shelter workers would pull a rope that raised a gate at the back of Tramp's enclosure out to one of two big runs outside. It was a chance to stretch his legs and breathe in fresh air again. The runs were enclosed by a tall, wire-mesh fence, beyond which Tramp could see the road leading to the hills to their west.

A little of the snow had settled on the ground, and it was too cold just to stand at the fence. Looking at the pile of outdoor toys, Tramp chose a deflated football, which he began pushing around with his nose. The activity helped take his mind off the frustration of being so close to home yet unable to complete the journey.

Of course, it would have been more fun if there were another dog to play with, but the shelter only let two dogs out together when they were positive that they would get along safely. Tramp grabbed the ball in his jaws and shook it from side to side. The ball flew away, and Tramp pounced after it. It landed right next to the fence, on the side where construction had begun for the new wing of the shelter (but had been halted during the bad weather). As Tramp lunged for the ball like a hunter for its prey, his snout pushed it against the bottom of the fence and it wedged further underneath. One of the metal brackets that held the wire mesh to a post had come off – perhaps it had been knocked during the construction work. It meant that there was more give in the fence than usual, enough give for the ball to make the fence bulge out at the bottom and create a slight gap. Tramp looked down at it in curiosity. The question was – was it enough of a gap?

There was no time to find out. The door back into the shelter building opened and he heard the clang of a food tray, accompanied by a 'Come here' whistle. There was no time for him to do anything. He padded back inside the building thoughtfully.

No doubt Tramp should have taken his time with the food in his bowl. After all, what was he going to do after he had eaten? But he had been hungry so often in the last few months that he couldn't stop himself from wolfing the food down at top speed.

He was just giving in to the usual after-meal drowsiness when the door to the dog section opened. As usual, the dogs at that end began to bark, and the barking spread from enclosure to enclosure like a wave.

'Be quiet, you lot!' said Lisa, then more quietly once the worst of the barking had died down, 'I'll just leave you to have a look around and get to know our dogs.'

The shuffle of feet indicated that there were a few other people with her.

'Thank you,' said a man's voice.

The door opened and shut again as Lisa left.

'Now remember, sweets,' said a woman's voice, 'we don't have to adopt a dog today, OK? We can come back lots of times until we find just the right one.'

'OK, Mum,' replied a girl's voice.

The footsteps grew louder and a moment later Tramp saw a young girl and her parents moving along the walkway between the two rows of enclosures. The girl went from cage to cage, giving each occupant a solemn look.

Tramp heard her reach the end of the room and turn back. She stopped again in front of the enclosure opposite Tramp's, the one that held Toby, the little cocker spaniel.

'I like this one,' the girl said. 'I like those long, floppy ears!'

Her parents joined her at the enclosure opposite Tramp. Toby lifted his head with a whimper of hopeful curiosity.

'It's not a puppy,' said her dad.

'He's a he, not an it,' corrected the girl, pointing to the card attached to the front of the dog's enclosure. 'And he's six.'

'It does say he's got a nice temperament,' added the girl's mum.

'Let's just have a proper look at the others,' said her dad. 'Choosing a dog is an important decision. It's not like just picking out a toy. This is like getting a new member of the family.'

But the girl wasn't listening. She had turned and was looking right at Tramp. 'No, wait,' she said. 'This is the one! Look at him! This is exactly the sort of dog I wanted.'

The girl's parents turned their attention to Tramp.

'It says that this one isn't available for adoption,' said her mum.

'But he looks really nice!' said the girl. 'And smart, too! Look at his eyes!'

'He probably isn't available *yet*, that's all,' said her dad. 'I bet we'll be able to come back in a few days and he will be.'

Tramp lay and listened carefully as the family talked. He didn't understand everything that was said, of course, but he remembered enough about how this sort of place worked. You were here for what seemed like forever, but then – if you were one of the lucky ones – a family came and took you away from this place. The way this family was talking now reminded him of how the Robbins family had adopted him from the shelter back when he was just a puppy.

But then he glimpsed Toby in the enclosure across the way. The spaniel lay with his head on the ground, his sad eyes looking up at the family.

Tramp was not the kind of dog that would do anything to harm a human. He would never do anything to threaten a human. But there were times when you had to do something that truly went against your own nature and now was just such a time.

Tramp began to growl. He hated to do it, but he forced himself to carry on. It wasn't loud, just a low rumble in the dog's throat, but that made it all the more threatening. Despite the locked door between them, the man took a step back. Tramp let the growl build into a sharp bark. It was Toby's only chance. The girl's eyes opened in alarm.

'I don't think this one would make a very good pet,' said her mother. Her husband shook his head in agreement.

It was only then that Tramp realized Lisa had rejoined the family.

The girl's father turned to her now. 'We'd like to know a little more about the spaniel,' he said.

'About Toby!' said the girl enthusiastically.

Lisa started to tell them all about what a friendly, good-natured dog Toby was, but before she did, she threw a worried frown in Tramp's direction. A troubling thought passed through her mind. Maybe the police report was right. Maybe this dog was a biter?

Chapter 8

Early the next morning, around the time he would usually be getting up, Joe sat at the television studio.

'Ready in about ten minutes, OK?' said a man with headphones and a clipboard. Joe nodded and took another sip of water.

His excitement about being at the local television station was diminished by how early in the morning he'd had to get here. It had still been dark when he and his mum had set out in the car.

His mum fussed with his hair once again.

'It's fine, Mum,' he said, pulling his head away.

'Just relax and be yourself,' she continued.

Joe nervously fingered the microphone that had been pinned to his sweater. He watched as the weatherman in the studio gave the local forecast for the next few days.

The man was standing in front of
nothing but a big blue screen, but Joe saw on
a monitor that it looked as if he was
actually standing in front of a weather map.

'No snow this far west yet,' the weatherman said, 'but they've already had the first
snowfall east of Woodford. And plenty more

61

is expected – there'll be a winter storm warning, in effect – and it's going to be heading our way. So make sure you dig out your snow boots!'

The station cut to advertisements. While they were off air, the producer led Joe to the desk where he would be interviewed. It was strange to meet the presenter, whose face Joe had seen so often on TV.

The presenter winked at Joe. 'It'll be over before you know it, kid,' he said.

And then the producer was counting down the seconds until they were back on air and Joe was suddenly aware of the huge TV camera trained on him.

'We've all heard stories about amazing pets,' said the presenter straight to the camera, 'but our next guest, Joe Robbins, can top them all.' He turned to Joe. 'Tell us what happened when you were on holiday this last spring.'

Joe took a deep breath and began to tell the story of how he and Tramp had been parted in the caves all those months ago. As he did so, his nerves melted away and he forgot about the TV camera.

'And you thought you'd lost him forever?'

'I thought he was dead,' answered Joe. Even though he'd told himself that he wouldn't go all blubbery, tears stung his eyes at the memory. He blinked them back.

'But months later you found out that Tramp wasn't dead,' prompted the presenter. 'Tell us how that happened.'

Joe explained how he had seen Tramp on a news report, how he had been sure it was the same dog. He gave the address of the website his mum had set up, and he held a photo of Tramp up to the camera. It showed the dog with a frisbee in his mouth, ready to play. Joe's fingers shook as he held the photo, but the cameraman still managed to get a good close-up.

And then the presenter was wishing him good luck and the interview was over.

'Is that it?' Joe asked, as his microphone was unclipped.

'That's it,' said the producer with a smile.

'Well, just one other thing,' she added. 'I know what it's like to lose a pet. I want to wish you the best of luck finding your dog! I really hope being on TV like this helps.'

Me too, thought Joe. Me too.

The last place Jimmy had expected to be before the holidays was inside a hospital in this part of the country.

It was amazing to him that he didn't have more serious injuries. The doctor at the hospital said he'd suffered a bad concussion – he hadn't even woken for forty-eight hours (though apparently he'd sung a few rock songs in his sleep!). He knew that he'd had a lucky escape in the crash. He had plenty of cuts and bruises, but nothing too serious.

Jimmy had called his sister on the phone and explained that, all being well, he'd be able to leave the hospital the next day, after just a few more tests.

'It's a good thing you only hit your head,' she said, when she knew that he was going to be OK. 'You don't use it for much anyway, do you?'

'Ha, ha,' Jimmy had replied, something he had said regularly to his big sister through-out their childhood.

With time to kill, he wandered to the TV room. Jimmy had wanted to watch music videos, but the two other patients outvoted him. That was the only reason why he ended up watching the morning news programme.

He kept half an eye on the news and weather, idly flicking through one of the many out-of-date magazines on the coffee table.

He was vaguely aware that the presenter was talking to a boy on the programme now, something about a missing dog . . .

And then Jimmy looked up and saw the photograph that filled the screen. He could hardly believe his eyes.

'Rocker!' he exclaimed. 'That dog's
Rocker!'

One of the other patients had picked up
the remote control and was aiming it at the
TV. 'I want to find the basketball results,'
he mumbled.

'No!' yelled Jimmy. 'Don't change the
channel!'

He leaned forwards and listened intently as Joe Robbins told the story of Tramp the dog, also known as Rocker.

Five minutes later, Jimmy was heading back to the telephone.

Chapter 9

In school, it was the last day of term — the last day of the whole year — and there was a buzz of excitement in the air.

Joe's arrival halfway through the morning had only added to the excitement. Lots of kids in the school had seen him on TV that morning. Several told him that they had videotaped it, in case Joe wanted to see what he looked like on screen. (In fact, Joe's big sister, Catherine, had taped the segment too.) One or two kids took the opportunity to poke fun — pretending to cry and wailing

'Oh, my poor little doggy!' – but most were sympathetic and encouraging.

After lunch, Joe's teacher abandoned all pretence of getting any work done. He had allowed the class to bring in board games or books, and there was a hubbub of happy activity in the classroom.

Joe joined in a game, but it was impossible to concentrate. He kept wondering if anyone had called in with information about Tramp. So when the intercom crackled, 'Joe Robbins, please come to the school office,' he leapt up so quickly that he almost knocked the board game flying. He made his way to the school office as quickly as he could, without actually running in the corridors.

Joe was surprised to find his mum waiting for him in the office.

'Get your coat,' she told him. 'You're leaving early.'

'What is it?' he asked. 'Is something the matter?'

His mum shook her head and smiled, but her eyes shone with tears. Joe thought he could hear the anxiety in her voice.

'It's Tramp,' she said. 'I think we may have found where he is.'

Joe's heart didn't just jump, it did a triple somersault! Could this be true?

'Where?' he asked. He knew that a big stupid grin was plastered on his face and he didn't mind one little bit.

'We think he's in the animal shelter over in Marshall County,' she said.

Marshall! The town of Marshall wasn't far away from them at all! That meant that Tramp had almost completed his long journey home.

'Did you call them to make sure?' he asked, trying to ignore the excited thudding of his heart.

'There's a bit of a problem. Some of the telephone lines are down around Marshall,' said his mum. 'It must be the winter storm blowing through. I kept trying but I could only get an automated message from the operator. But don't worry . . . Even in the bad weather, we can drive over there within an hour.'

Joe gave a vigorous nod of the head. 'So what are we waiting for?'

On the drive over, Joe's mum explained what she knew about the situation. As far as she could tell, Tramp had been in a vehicle that was involved in a crash on the highway.

'He wasn't hurt, was he?' asked Joe worriedly.

'No,' said Mum. 'Well, I don't think he was.'

She went on to tell how the man in the accident had been in a nearby hospital. He had tried already to find out what had happened to Tramp, and the local police department had promised to get back to him. But then he had seen Joe on the morning news and he had instantly recognized Tramp's photograph. His next telephone call had begun a chain of hurried calls — the Marshall police department, the television station and finally the Robbins' house. Piecing the information together like a jigsaw puzzle, Joe's mum realized that the police officer had thought that Tramp had caused the accident. She knew that he had been taken to the shelter. But then she wasn't able to telephone the shelter to confirm this. Nor could the police send an officer over to the shelter – with a big storm on the way, they couldn't spare anyone until the next day at the very earliest. No, the easiest thing was for Joe and his mum just to drive there themselves.

The further east they went, the darker and darker the sky became with towering grey clouds. There was plenty of snow at the side of the highway here, but it looked as if the forecast had been right – there was a lot more on the way.

As Mum took the Marshall exit off the highway, the snow had begun to fall, and by the time they reached the animal shelter, it was falling heavily.

The woman at the front desk in the reception area wore a name badge that said BECCA on it, and it looked brand new. She seemed flustered as she flicked through a stack of papers on the front desk.

'I'm sorry to keep you waiting,' she said at last to Joe and his mum. 'Things are a bit chaotic, I'm afraid. This is my first week working here – I'm not really meant to be here on my own but Lisa the shelter director hasn't made it in. She lives up over Middleton way and I think the roads there might be closed because of the storm. But I can't check because our phones aren't even working.' There was a note of panic in her voice.

Joe's mum explained that they had been told that Tramp was here and she gave a quick description of the family pet.

Becca nodded quickly. 'Yes, I'm sure we've got a dog that fits that description. Come this way.'

They followed Becca to the dog area. The barks that erupted when the door opened were louder than ever, probably because their food was late in coming today.

Becca walked along to Tramp's enclosure ... and froze. It was empty.

Frowning, Becca rushed along to the window at the end of the walkway and looked out to the dog runs outside. But they too were empty.

'I . . . don't understand,' said Becca.

A chill of unease ran down Joe's spine. Something was wrong.

'Perhaps he's been moved to another enclosure,' suggested Joe's mum. But it only took a minute or two to check that this wasn't the case.

Back at the front desk, Becca rifled through the shelter's paperwork.

'He hasn't been adopted by someone, has he?' asked Joe's mum.

'No, I'm sure he hasn't. I'd have a record of that right here . . .' Becca suddenly looked up, a look of pale horror on her face. 'Unless . . .'

'Yes?'

'The dog you're looking for, we were told he might be dangerous.'

Joe's mum nodded. 'Yes, that was just a misunderstanding. They thought that Tramp had caused the accident, but he didn't.'

But the grim look didn't leave Becca's face. 'Well he definitely hasn't been adopted. The only thing I can think is . . . They must have needed the space for another dog. I . . . I'm afraid he must have been put to sleep . . . I'm so sorry.'

She began to explain how the shelter hardly ever put dogs down, and on the few occasions they did, the method – an injection – was swift and painless. But Joe didn't hear the rest of the woman's explanation. He didn't notice his mum's arm around his shoulders. The terrible words echoed in his mind. Put to sleep! Only it wasn't to sleep, was it? His dog had been put down forever. It wasn't fair! Tramp had travelled such a great distance; he had battled almost the entire way home.

And now, after all that and with such a little way to go, Tramp was dead!

Chapter 10

There were so many ifs. If Becca hadn't been new at the shelter . . . If the phones had been working around Marshall . . . If the storm hadn't prevented Lisa from making it to the shelter as she usually did . . . If any of these things had happened, they would have been able to work out the truth of the matter right away.

In fact, Tramp was cold and he was hungry and tired . . . and he was very much alive.

When he had been let out into the dog run late that morning, he ran straight to the

far side of the fence, where he found the
broken section with the deflated football still
wedged under the mesh. He drove it further
in, and then he began to dig away at
the earth with his front paws. The cold
ground was hard, but once the top layer
was gone, it became a little easier. At any

moment, he expected a voice to shout at him, but none did.

At last, the gap beneath the fence seemed big enough for him to squeeze his head through. Then came the hard part. It seemed impossible that he would get his shoulders through as well. The sharp points of the bottom of the fence dug into him, but Tramp wriggled and crawled, dismissing the pain as the fence scraped along his back. He was making it! He thought that the worst might be over when he'd got his chest through, but he hadn't anticipated how much his damaged back leg would hurt when he pulled it through. The pain was terrible, but there was no way he could go back now. Stifling a howl of pain, he hauled himself through.

And then he was standing on the other side of the fence. The wind was bitter, but to Tramp at that moment it felt wonderful. He had done it! But he knew that he couldn't hang around here congratulating himself. He ran for the shelter of the trees ahead, and then on westward.

He was feeling well rested and strong at first, but the cold in the air soon sapped his energy. There was quite a lot of snow still on the ground. Soon the pads of his feet were numb with the cold.

But on he ran. He wouldn't let himself stop, not now, when he was so close to home. When he needed a drink he simply bent his head down to lap up snow.

At first Tramp followed the line of the highway, before veering off to the hills to one side. This route would cut a long way off the rest of the journey. What Tramp didn't know was that, even as he was moving away from the highway, Joe and his mum were joining the very same road just a few miles to the east.

The dog battled on all afternoon. The

terrain was uneven and occasionally he wandered into snowdrifts that he had to push his way through. The going got harder still when the snow began to fall again. As evening came, the snow did not abate. It seemed to bathe everything in a cold, blue light, muffling all sounds in the forest around him, so that he began to feel like the loneliest creature on the planet.

As the hours went by, Tramp's tiredness grew and grew until it blotted out almost every thought in his mind. The only one he could hold on to was the one that kept him going – home! Though his legs ached with weariness and were numb with cold, he knew that each step was taking him closer and closer to home.

It was more and more difficult to judge the snow's depth, and the blanket of white concealed various logs and bushes that tripped him. But whenever Tramp tumbled forwards into the snow, he pulled himself to his feet again. It seemed as if the snow would keep falling forever, that this was what the entire world consisted of now – the night, the woods and the falling snow.

But eventually, it began to subside and then finally stop. And when it did, Tramp saw a wonderful sight in the distance below. It was the lights of a town –

his town! One of those lights glittering below belonged to the house that was *his* home!

The sight gave him a fresh surge of energy. At last Tramp was at the foot of the

hills and the ground under the snow was
once again pavement. Now he trotted under
the glare of street lights, running from one
pool of orange light to the next. It was
late by now, and he heard only a few cars

in the distance. None passed him.

Part of Tramp's mind was insisting that he should just have a bit of a rest, but he knew that if he lay down now, he might not be able to get up again. His body was wracked with cold and pain.

But he was still able to lift his head and sniff the air. He was rewarded with a flood of familiar smells. He was close to his old neighbourhood. The familiar sights and smells gave him another tiny burst of energy. Memories crowded in as he made his way past place after place – here was the bakery where Catherine had dropped a doughnut and Tramp had gobbled it up; here was the entrance to the dog park he had run around so many times.

It was a huge effort to lift his paws now – his legs felt as if they were lead – but he turned one corner, crossed the street and turned another. He was nearly there. Tramp's walk had become a stagger now, but he just had to keep going another couple of blocks.

He heard the sound of speeding feet, muffled by the snow, and then he caught the scent of an old enemy. It was Fritz! Fritz the Dobermann, the dog who had delighted in chasing and bullying him ever since Tramp had been a puppy.

The big dog's owners usually let him out late at night. Fritz was often content to stay in the yard, but if something beyond the fence attracted his attention, he didn't have much difficulty getting out. The smell of another dog in the neighbourhood was more than enough to get Fritz going. As he raced towards Tramp now, he looked more like a guard dog than a pet.

Once there had been a time when the very mention of Fritz's name would have caused Tramp to cower or run. Not any more. As the Dobermann raced towards

him, Tramp held his ground, and it wasn't fatigue that stopped him from fleeing. He was a different dog now. He had survived constant hunger and treacherous rivers and raging fires. He had faced coyotes and dogs and snakes and he had faced people who hated strays like him, and he had survived them all. Fritz didn't seem like much of a problem in comparison.

When the big dog was almost upon him, Tramp let out a bark. It wasn't especially loud, but somehow that bark contained all of the frustration Tramp had felt on his long journey home, and all of the inner strength that he had built up, too, over those long, long months.

Fritz pulled up fast, wagging his stubby tail in nervous confusion. His nose told him that he knew this dog, but there was something about it that made him uneasy. He gave a gruff little bark, mostly for show, and then turned round and ran back to his own house.

Tramp was almost done. He tottered forwards. Chains of Christmas lights in a few houses lit the street. They seemed to dance and blur in front of Tramp's eyes. His head seemed to be spinning.

But the house was there, just up ahead. He could see it, could imagine the cosy smell of it, the look of every single room.

He took a final step, wobbled, and then collapsed.

Chapter 11

Mum and Joe had had to remain in Marshall for the rest of the evening because the snow had closed down a stretch of the highway. At first, they'd thought that they would have to stay in a motel, but it said on the radio that the storm would end fairly quickly. Once fresh snow stopped falling, the snowploughs would quickly make the highway accessible again.

And so it was late when they finally drove home. Joe was silent in the back seat, but Mum knew that he wasn't sleeping. She

tried to think of something to say, anything
that could comfort him, but the words
would not come.

It was close to midnight when they
turned off to the streets of Woodford. The
smaller roads still hadn't been ploughed.

'I don't think I can get the car up our

street,' said Mum, when they came to the foot of the hill that they lived halfway up.

'I'll have to go the long way round.'

'Can I get out and walk?' asked Joe. These were the first words he'd said in over an hour.

The house was in sight from here and

Mum knew that Dad and Catherine would be home and waiting up. She nodded.

The snow crunched under Joe's feet. He had no gloves or scarf on, and the cold air stung his hands and face, but he didn't care. He looked up at the night-time sky. The clouds had begun to part and, even amidst the glow of Christmas lights, he could make out a few stars. When he saw the solitary North Star, a sob escaped him. He could remember sitting outside with Tramp on many an evening, looking up at the stars, pointing out that one in particular.

He would never be able to do that again.

Suddenly he saw something up ahead, an animal. It was lying in the snow between the sidewalk and the street. A racoon, perhaps? Whatever it was, it wasn't moving. Was it dead? Joe slowed down, ready go wide around the animal.

But then Joe realized that this wasn't a

racoon. It was a dog, but it wasn't just any old dog. He got closer and . . .

'Tramp!'

Was it a trick? Were his eyes just showing him the one thing in the world he most wanted to see? No, it was true! The dog was really here. Tramp was really here. Joe began to race forwards.

Meanwhile, Tramp's dreams were nothing

but cold, a more terrible coldness than any he had ever known. He no longer had the energy to fight; he just let himself be carried by it, as if he were swept along on a sea of cold.

But then a voice drifted across that sea, pulling him back.

'Tramp!'

How long had it been since he had heard that name? How long since he had heard that voice?

With effort Tramp's eyes slowly opened. He was still lying on the snow-covered ground, but someone was kneeling over him.

It was Joe! Tears were streaming down the boy's face, tears of disbelief and happiness. Tramp let out a gentle bark, full of relief at being home, at being back where he was supposed to be. Back with Joe!

He had hoped for this moment for so

long that it hardly seemed real, but it *was* real, because then the boy was hugging Tramp and pressing his face into the side of the dog's neck, and Tramp was licking Joe's laughing face.

The two were still this way when Mum's car pulled into the driveway up ahead. They were still hugging and laughing when Dad and Catherine joined Mum at the front door to witness the amazing sight.

Finally, Joe stood up. Tramp got to his feet too, but Joe just smiled. Bending down he scooped the dog up, cradling him in both arms. 'You don't have to make it on your own,' he said. 'Not now.'

Joe started towards the house. 'Let's go home.'

Early the next morning, Tramp dreamed that his belly was full and he was in a lovely, warm place where he was with the ones he

loved and who
loved him, and
when he half
opened his eyes
he saw that it
wasn't a dream
at all. He was
home – home!
– and there was
Joe, in his own
bed with a look
of contented peace on his sleeping face.

After all these months of weary loneliness, Tramp was back with his master. They
would be able to run together through the

park! If there was still enough snow on the ground, Joe might go sledging on the hill at the golf course and Tramp could charge after the sledge as he always did! Or they could play catch with any of Tramp's wide assortment of tennis balls, frisbees and chewed-up toys!

The dog looked at the sleeping boy. There was so much they could do now they were together again, but there'd be plenty of time for all that. For now, it was hard to say no to just a little more rest after such a very long journey. Tramp flopped back down into his nice warm basket, right next to Joe's bed, and let sleep wrap its tender arms around him once again.